This story is for my two daughters, Catriona Faraday-White and Alice Faraday-Dempsey. Their continuous support makes everything worthwhile.

Acknowledgements

My grateful thanks must once again go to Ruth Midgley, my brother-in-law Ruairidh Greig, and cousins David and Mary Shaw, for their many helpful suggestions and invaluable assistance in proofreading the script.

About the Author

Ian Faraday was born in Morecambe, England and moved to Sheffield in 1969 to train as a teacher, specializing in French and Music. Most of his teaching career was spent working with children of primary age. During this time he began writing songs for annual school productions. A number of his works have been published.

Ian has always enjoyed children's literature, and 'Beyond The Magic Path' follows the publication of 'The Magic Path', his first story in this series.

He has two daughters and two grandchildren. His main interests other than writing are playing the piano and working in Youth Theatre.

Kat Geraldson always enjoyed going to school. She also enjoyed going home. There, she could be in her own room and shut out the rest of the world for a little while. She could change out of her school uniform into her jeans and T-shirt and relax. Her favourite pastimes were listening to music or playing video games on her laptop. Sometimes, she had text conversations with friends, and often, these went on for quite a while, only having to be cut short if there was homework to be done!

Today, Kat left school accompanied by her best friend, Nick Thomas, who was in the same class. She appeared to be in a particularly good mood! The reason was that tomorrow, Tuesday 14th of June, would be her eleventh birthday, and, as an early treat, for tea tonight, her Mum and dad were preparing chicken and chips! Nick was the only guest at this meal, but tomorrow, several of her friends had been invited to a local pizza restaurant for a birthday celebration, something she was greatly looking forward to.

Just as exciting was the thought of a particular video game, 'Legend of Legends,' which she had asked for as her main birthday present. The children crossed the playground together and climbed the small flight of steps that led to the school gate. From there, they began the short walk back home.

The pavement was flagged, and they played their usual game of hopping from one paving stone to another without touching the cracks in between! There was some intense competition here, but much laughter and accusation when one or both of them failed the challenge! Within a few minutes they reached Kat's house and parted company, Nick not having far to go, as he lived next door! She went in and, as usual, said 'hi' to her Mum, who was in the kitchen cutting up potatoes to make real chips. She hung up her coat in the hall and headed straight upstairs to her room. After changing out of her school uniform, she sat on her bed, mobile phone in hand. She wanted to text Nick with the idea that a walk would be good fun, to build up an appetite before tea - and she knew exactly where she wanted to go!

The children's favourite route to the village centre ran behind their houses and was known to them as the 'magic path.' This leafy track had recently led them to two amazing adventures, as it had an incredible, magical power that could guide them to different periods in time - and when they were not expecting it! They often talked together about their time travels, but they had never shared their experiences with family or friends. There was no proof of what had happened to them, and they felt that no one would ever believe their story. Only they knew the truth.

Nick replied immediately to Kat's text and said he would call round at five o'clock.

The special tea was at six today, a little later than usual, so there was just enough time for a wander up and down the magic path before they were expected home.

Late afternoon sunshine warmed their backs as they made their way to its entrance, which was just down the road from where they lived. Every time they used the path, they wondered whether a further adventure might be imminent, but they also knew full well that no matter how much they wanted this, it might never happen again. The path would give up its secrets when it was ready!

After they had walked a short distance, they stopped for their customary look at the stream, which ran next to the path. Unfortunately, it had lately become clogged with broken branches and twigs, causing its flow to be temporarily reduced in some places. For a few seconds, they were captivated by the slowly moving water until a sudden rustling sound caused them to look around. They were surprised to see a grey squirrel jumping out from behind a laurel bush and landing in front of them. Turning away, it skipped towards the trunk of a tall, ivy-covered oak tree and scrambled to the end of one of the branches. Discovering it could go no further, it returned to the main trunk, where it was joined by a sprightly second squirrel.

They chased each other down the trunk to the ground, where, for a second, they stared up at Kat and Nick with a quizzical look on their faces. It was almost as if they were inviting the children to go with them before they disappeared along a narrow track leading off into the undergrowth. Kat and Nick had never noticed this track before, as it was almost completely hidden by vegetation. Two felled tree trunks outlined where it started. The children's sense of adventure urged them to find out where it might lead, so they followed it through ferns, tall grass, and trees before bursting out into open ground.

A completely different scene to what they were expecting panned out in front of them. They were standing at the top of a valley, which sloped downwards and away from them for some distance.

Both its sides rose up to tree-lined, higher ground. Green fields, some populated by sheep and cows, stretched away into the distance. A river, on which a number of ducks were enjoying the warmth of the sun, flowed lazily past the nearest field. Here and there, workers were going about their daily farming tasks. Some must have been repairing hedges, and they were building a bonfire to burn the surplus branches and twigs. The children should have been looking at the familiar streets and houses of their own village, but they could see nothing more than five or six thatched cottages not far from where they were standing. These all had beamed walls and, from the outside, looked to have only a ground floor. There were no windows to be seen. Dotted around the cottages were a number of outhouses and one building that looked like a barn. Strangely, just at that moment, it became significantly colder in spite of the pleasant sunshine that bathed the valley. A breeze sprang up and wafted the chilly air around the children, causing them to shiver and wrap their arms around themselves.

From previous experiences, they were aware of what this drop in temperature meant and were now positive that they had travelled to a different time but had no idea where they were or what year it was. While wondering what to do next, the children heard the sound of galloping hooves.

This grew louder as they looked around to see where it was coming from. All of a sudden, a horse crashed out of a nearby copse of trees, pursued by two men, one carrying a rope. They were shouting the horse's name,

'Galahad,' and all three were heading straight towards Kat and Nick, who were not sure which way to jump to avoid a collision!

They raised their hands in a futile effort to protect themselves, resigned to the fact that they might be seriously injured. Remarkably, this did not happen.

Instead, Galahad came to a halt just beyond where they were standing and began munching the surrounding grass. The two men, however, ran straight *through* Kat and Nick's bodies as if there was nothing there and then stopped abruptly next to the horse. The children briefly felt a more intense cold as this happened. They were both breathing heavily, but they felt very relieved that they had avoided being trampled! Galahad approached the children and put his head near them, inviting them to stroke his nose. Kat took up the offer and ran her hand softly down his long and beautiful face.

She and Nick were speechless, as they knew that the first children they met at a different time would be able to see and interact with them. They did not know that they would also be visible to animals! This was quite a new discovery! The men looped a rope around Galahad's neck, wondering why he was showing no interest in them and how on earth he had quickly become so docile. They led him tamely across a neat

stone-block bridge and into one of the lower fields. He seemed much happier and had certainly forgotten about whatever had spooked him. He even turned his head towards Kat and Nick and nodded to them before they watched him being set free.

Such was their nature; Kat and Nick were now anxious to find out exactly where they were and what year it was. To do that, they would need to talk to other children, but until this moment, none had appeared. If any were here, they needed to be found.

As they approached the nearest cottage, a number of farm labourers, some carrying tools, were walking purposefully to and from the fields, clearly unaware of them.

Men and women walked around them and occasionally through them, which was still a cold and unsettling experience, although the children found themselves becoming increasingly more accustomed to it.

As they arrived at the first cottage, it was noticeable that the breeze had increased in strength, and the sun was now hiding behind grey clouds. Attached to the front wall of the cottage was a rough, wooden plaque, and painted on it was the number 1647.

This was probably the date the cottage had been built and gave them, at least, some idea of the period they were in. The sound of a loud crash and raised voices persuaded them to peer into the interior through the open front door. In the dimness, they could make out a single, large room, in which they noticed a wooden table and four stools.

An open fireplace, with a cooking pot suspended over a log fire, could be seen across the earthen floor. The children were thinking how gloomy it all looked when a boy and a girl emerged from the shadows on the far side of the room.

Secrets of the Magic Path

The boy was wearing a waistcoat over his shirt, and his trousers ended below the knee.

The girl had on a brown dress with a white apron. Neither wore shoes. They looked to be about ten or eleven years old. Kat wanted to find out what had happened in there, so without hesitation, she tapped on the door and went in, confident that these children would see her and that she would be able to talk to them. Nick followed behind.

'Sorry, the door was open.' Kat apologised for their uninvited entry. As expected, the boy immediately noticed their presence.

'Who are you?' he asked. 'We've not seen you in Tangleford Valley before,' he added. The tone of his voice was friendly but cautious. Kat had already invented a story to cover their arrival.

'We were passing your cottage on our way to the fields,' she said, 'when we heard a loud noise. We just wanted to check you were alright. My name is Katherine, and this is Nicholas. Our friends call us Kat and Nick.'

'The noise?' said the boy, 'oh, that is nothing to worry about. My sister Alice was clearing some plates and things from the table, and she dropped the tray. What a fuss she made! By the way, I'm Richard Fletcher, and this is Alice.'

Kat and Nick, as on previous excursions through time, already felt comfortable and safe. A relaxed and cordial atmosphere filled the room. The four children seemed very pleased to have met each other and, remarkably, no comments were made about the obvious difference in their clothing, even though, if this was the 17th century, Kat and Nick's jeans and T-shirts were definitely out of place!

'We've only just come to live in the valley, at the top end,' began Kat, who was keen on giving some sort of reason why they had not met before. 'You're the first children we've seen,' she continued. Briefly, she hesitated, searching for something else to say.

Then she had an idea.

'Our parents are away for the day, so we've come out looking for a job - can your father help us? Does he work on the land?' she asked with a smile. Alice's face took on an expression of sadness, and she looked as though she was about to burst into tears.

With an effort, she pulled herself together.

'Our father died in the great plague two years ago in 1665,' she said with difficulty.

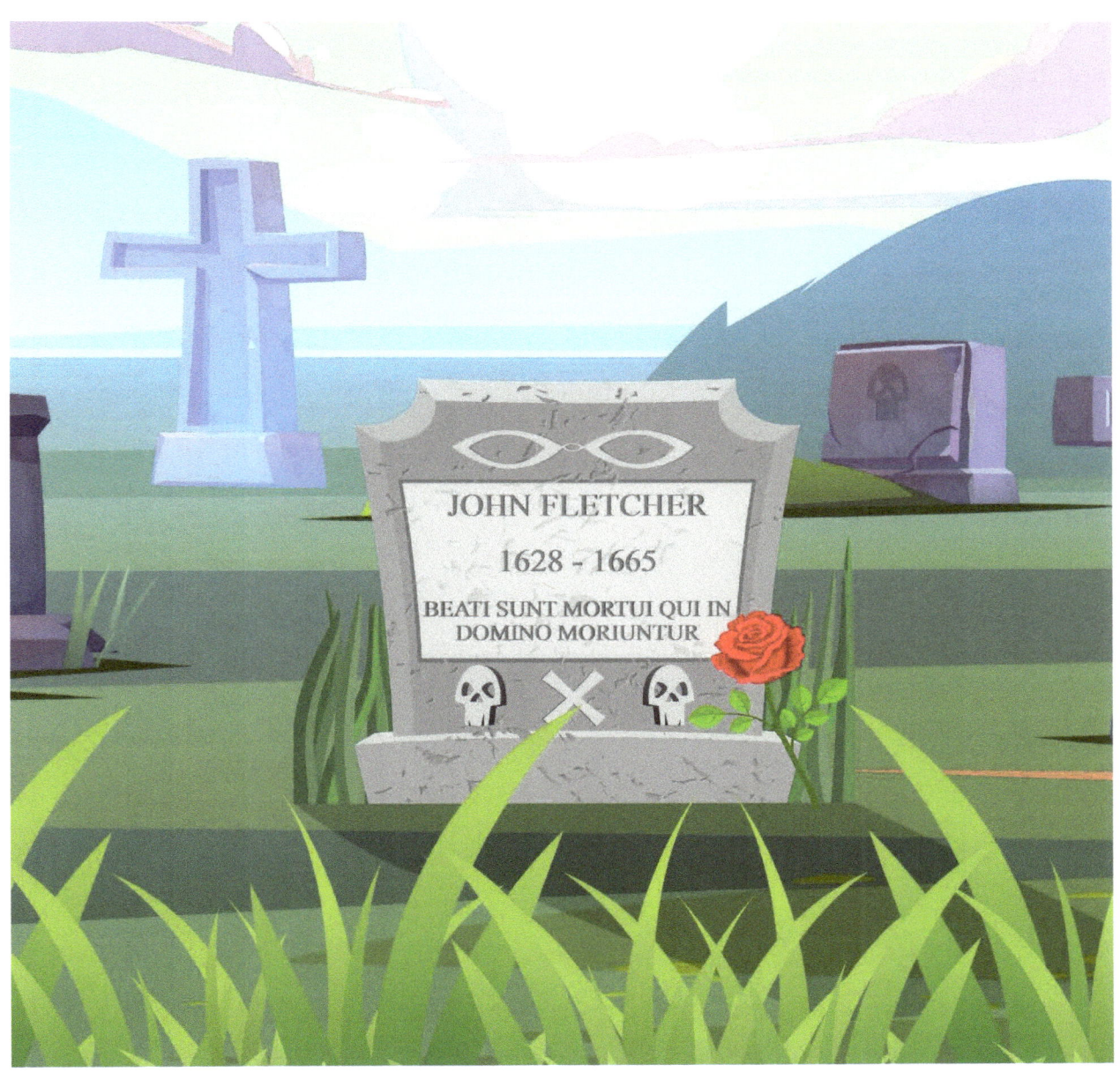

Kat and Nick immediately felt sorry for her but were grateful for this clue to the current date, which must be 1667. However, it also occurred to them that in order to avoid suspicion, they would need to come up with some ideas of their own experiences of the plague!

Alice went on, 'It spread here from London, and he fell ill very quickly. We don't know who he caught it from, but a lot of others died from it here in the valley and many more around the country, so we heard. Men, women and children, sometimes whole families, all gone so fast. Mother nursed him as best she could, but once the plague took hold, there was no cure.' Her eyes filled up with tears. Emotion prevented her from continuing, so Richard took over.

'We don't know how, but Mother did not get sick, and neither did we. We prayed every day that Father would get better. But he died. Why him and not us? At least the plague is over now, and things are getting back to normal.

There haven't been any new cases here since the summer of last year.' He paused. There was something else bothering him.

'How is it that you did not become ill?' he asked Kat, 'and what about your family?

Did they avoid the plague?'

The answer to these questions could have caused Kat and Nick some difficulties, but fortunately, they had already worked out what to say.

They had some knowledge of the Great Plague from a school project and had read that there were people who may have had a special gene in their body that protected them, and that might explain Richard, Alice, and their mother's survival. More important, as far as they were concerned, was that they also knew that those who could escape to the countryside to try and avoid infection. Nick dealt with the response.

'We stayed with friends in the north of England. They had a house in the country.

We weren't allowed out, and nobody else could come in. They had their own well for water, but food was difficult to find. We managed for a whole year, though!'

'Your family must have lots of money,' remarked Alice, 'I thought only rich people were able to do that!'

Kat and Nick both nodded and then laughed a little nervously, hoping that there wouldn't be any more awkward questions. Alice was about to continue speaking when there was a cough from the other side of the room.

'Come and meet our mother,' said Richard, 'she's not been well lately, but she's now on the road to recovery. There's a good story to tell about that!' He took Kat and Nick over to a bed. Sitting up in it was a woman who looked a little pale, but they did not get the impression that she was very ill.

'Here she is,' said Richard. He gently stroked his mother's hair before adjusting her covers. She smiled at her children, but unsurprisingly, she stared straight through Kat and Nick before asking for a drink, which Alice then brought to her.

'Thank you. I am feeling so much better today,' she said, 'and it's all due to you two. Your father would have been so proud of you.' Alice was eager to introduce her mother to the new friends she and her brother had made.

'We have brought some visitors to see you!' she said, excitedly pushing Kat and Nick to the front. Mrs Fletcher looked puzzled for a moment, and then she shifted her gaze to glance around the room. She spoke slowly.

'I don't see anyone else. What do you mean, visitors? There's nobody else here, just you and your sister!'

Now it was Richard and Alice's turn to be confused. Kat and Nick were standing next to them, plainly visible to them!

'It's true, mother,' insisted Richard, 'we met Katherine and Nicholas today. They have come to live in Tangleford Valley, and we want to be friends with them.'

'Don't be silly, Richard,' continued his mother, 'you're playing games with me.

Perhaps you've seen a ghost!' She smiled, then sighed and went on, 'I'm tired now, and I want to sleep. I will see you both later.' She lay back and closed her eyes.

None of the children were sure what to say about this extraordinary episode, so everyone stood quietly for a few seconds. Kat broke the silence.

'Perhaps she is still not completely recovered, and this is part of her illness,' she suggested.

'I think you're right, let's leave it there and let her rest,' remarked Nick. He wanted to end any guessing game without it getting too deep.

The four children looked expectantly at each other, but no other explanation was offered, so they went to sit down together at the table. Richard wanted to tell them 'the story' about what had been happening recently in their household.

'We have been looking after Mother since she fell ill two weeks ago,' he began.

'When people knew about this, a false rumour began to spread around the valley that the plague had returned, and she had caught it! No one came near the Fletcher's house at first; they were all unsure. But we had to do something to help mother. We had watched her nurse father, and we tried some of the remedies she had used on him.'

'We didn't have enough money to ask a doctor to visit,' added Alice, 'so we gave her 'simples,' made from herbs and plants out of the garden - sage, feverfew and lavender, and black pepper for her cough.

We had seen her use leeches to rid father of bad blood, but we weren't brave enough to do that!' She pulled a funny face before going on. 'There were never any serious signs of the plague. No rash, not a single blister! She had a fever and chills, so she took to her bed and slept a lot. She said she just needed to rest. We managed to give her a little food and drink.'

Kat was fascinated with these descriptions, but she couldn't help thinking about the bloodletting, which would have been a dangerous waste of time. She thought it pointless to try and explain this to Richard and Alice. With her limited knowledge of twenty-first-century medicine, she thought that the children's mother must have picked up a virus from somewhere, which manifested itself in some of the plague's early symptoms. There wouldn't have been any danger to others in the valley, as she was sure that the plague had virtually died out nearly everywhere by the summer of 1666, and the current year was 1667. She felt that the neighbours in the valley had deserted this family in their hour of need.

'So, when did other people start taking more interest in you all?' she asked rather pointedly.

Richard chuckled and answered the question with a cheeky grin on his face.

'I followed everyone else's example and spread my own rumour!' he said rather proudly. 'Mother started to improve after about a week, so at that point, I stood by the door for a while every day and told anyone who passed by how well she was! I even persuaded her to wave and smile at them all. It wasn't long before the word got around, and people realised that the plague rumours were not true. They soon started to visit and offer help, which we didn't actually need by then! They were all very apologetic!'

This made the children smile as they visualised the situation, but the humour was cut short. Nick stood up quickly and headed to the door.

'I smell smoke,' he said, with a troubled expression on his face, 'where is it coming from?'

They all went outside and ran towards the source of the smoke, which was the bonfire in the nearest field, where labourers were still burning the hedging waste. But that wasn't all.

While they had been talking, the breeze had become noticeably stronger and had blown debris and sparks through the air straight onto the thatched roof of one of the cottages. It had easily caught fire due to recent warm weather and a lack of rain in the area.

Amidst a great deal of shouting, people began scurrying backwards and forwards, some running straight through Kat and Nick as they rushed towards the blaze. Ladders were being placed against the cottage walls, and a human chain had formed between the river and the building. Buckets were passed along the chain until water could be thrown onto the thatch to soak and protect the areas of the roof that were not on fire. From earlier experiences, people here knew that thatch was very difficult to extinguish with water, so they had found other ways to put fires out. At the top of the ladders, some men with pitchforks were attempting to remove the burning sections of thatch. Others were trying to create a firebreak by cutting a channel into it. Some progress was being made when things took a distinct turn for the worse. A strong gust of wind blew clouds of sparks into the air and straight onto the roofs of two more cottages. The thatch on these quickly burst into flames, which then spread down the wattle and daub walls to the easily combustible tar-soaked beams. Kat and Nick wanted to offer help if they could, but as they turned towards their friends, they saw a look of horror on both Richard's and Alice's faces.

'That's our house on fire!' screamed Alice, clearly terrified and pointing at the flickering flames on its roof, 'and our mother is still in there, asleep! We have to get her out.'

They needed to move fast. The four of them raced back to the burning cottage.

A lot of people were already there and had begun to tackle the spreading flames.

'We have to go in!' shouted Richard, 'our mother is in there, we have to go in, we have to go in!' he yelled in panic.

The flames had already reached the doorway when a woman confronted them, trying to explain how dangerous it would be to enter the house. She attempted to restrain Richard, grabbing him by the arm, but he was in no mood for an argument, and he broke away, giving her a hefty kick in the shins. While the woman was clutching her leg and hobbling around in pain, the four children went in through the front door. There was smoke in the interior, and they could hear loud coughing coming from the far side of the room. Their eyes were streaming, and it was becoming more difficult to breathe. They reached their mother's bed, and she was sitting up, her hand over her mouth, trying hard to control her coughing. She had only just woken up and was confused as she tried to work out what was happening.

'Mother, you need to come with us, NOW!' shouted Alice as she threw back the bed covers. Her children helped her to stand. Kat and Nick could do nothing.

They tried to offer assistance, but their hands simply passed through the woman's body, as had been the case with everyone apart from Alice and Richard. They stood back, feeling frustrated and totally helpless.

'What is happening?' asked their mother anxiously.

'We can't explain now!' yelled Richard. 'There's a fire, so we are going to help you out of here. Come on, Mother, you have to try as well!'

Her children stood on either side of her, each holding one of her arms for support. As they all struggled towards the door, on the other side of the room, part of the burning roof fell in, coming down onto the bed where their mother had been resting. They could hear people shouting to them at the entrance, urging them to get out before it was too late. Two men tried to reach them, but their rescue attempts failed as flames now engulfed the doorway. The fire had now taken hold all around, blocking their way out, and with the smoke and heat becoming unbearable, they were beginning to think that their chances of survival were ebbing away. Suddenly, Richard stood still and shouted at the top of his voice.

'Follow me! I know how we might get out!' His words gave them hope, but Kat and Nick were unsure what he meant. He led them towards the back of the room, where they saw what looked like some sort of fence separating the living area from the space behind it. So, what was this fence for? Nick glanced over it and came face to face with the last thing he was expecting - a large and very confused pig! There was no time for questions as Alice pulled open a wicker gate, which led into what they now realised was an indoor animal pen. In they went, with Richard and Alice leading their mother.

'There's a small door in the wall - look, you can see it there!' called out Richard. Through the smoke, they saw what he was pointing towards. It was extremely lucky that the fire had not spread there yet, but it wouldn't be long before that happened.

"Who are you talking to?' asked a puzzled Mrs Fletcher, shaking her head.

'Our friends, Katherine and Nicholas. I told you about them before! They are trying to help us,' replied Richard. He quickly turned towards them.

'We can't let go of Mother,' he said, 'so you two are going to have to undo the latch on the door to let us out. It's always a bit awkward – and very stiff, but once you've pulled it up, the door should swing open.'

Nick moved quickly to the door and tried to grasp the latch. He made an attempt to pull it upwards, but nothing happened. Above, the crackle of fire and flames was growing louder, and although there was less smoke in this area, the heat was becoming intense. There was no way that they could go back - this was their only exit.

'Try again!' shouted Kat. She was hoping that the effort of shifting a stubborn door latch was not too much for a visitor to 1667!

'Come on, come on! Hurry!' called out Alice. There was an element of panic in her voice. 'It will move, but you must push a lot harder!' she went on. At this, her mother shook her head, still straining to discover who Alice was talking to, as she could only see her own two children.

'It might move if we work together!' shouted Kat. 'I'm coming over!'

Kat joined him and together they made a third attempt to take hold of the latch, and this time it moved, firstly slowly, but then it suddenly became free! They were able to force the door open, almost falling outside through the gap, followed by Alice, Richard, and their mother.

'Clover, you too!' yelled Richard to the family pig, which needed little encouragement to vacate its living quarters. It sped outside, bumping into Nick and squealing as it made its exit before disappearing into the distance.

He had to smile at Kat, as this second encounter with an animal was ample proof that the first *children* they met were not the only ones to be aware of their existence in a different time! The Fletchers would find Clover later.

After the smoke-filled room, the fresh air out in the open came as a huge relief. They stood for a moment, sucking it in and breathing deeply before moving quickly away from the danger. There were some straw bales at a safe distance for their mother to sit on while they watched the surrounding frantic activity.

The blaze had virtually been extinguished, as far as the first two cottages were concerned, but tragically, there was no chance of saving the Fletcher's house. Just as disastrous, no contents could be salvaged.

All they could do was watch while the cottage and everything in it rapidly burned to the ground. At that point, people with buckets of water began damping down the embers.

Distraught, the children sat with their mother, staring blankly at the ruins of their home as friends came to them to offer comfort and help. First their father and now this - life had not been kind to this family.

The wind strength had now dropped, leaving the strong smell of burnt wood and smoke to linger in the air. Kat tried to find words to say how sorry she was. It was difficult.

'I wish there was something we could do,' she said to Richard, as she touched his arm, 'but there isn't,' she added sadly.

'I don't think there is either,' he replied with a sigh.

'Don't think there is what?' interrupted his mother, who thought he was addressing her. She went on, almost angrily, 'We'll just have to start again with nothing, maybe even leave Tangleford Valley. Oh, I do wish your father were here.' Tears began to trickle down her cheeks, and she buried her face in her hands.

'You won't have to start again by yourself,' came a voice from somewhere behind them.

They stood up from the straw bale and turned round to see that a group of people had gathered. Two or three were carrying pitchforks, and they all had dirty clothes and faces, having come from the fire. The voice was that of an older man who stood at the front and spoke again.

'We let you down when you were ill, and we are all very sorry for that. We aim to make it up to you.' He paused as the rest of the group murmured their unanimous agreement. 'We will all help you to rebuild your home, and until it is ready, there are many who have offered to let you stay with them here in the valley. We will look after you, all of you. You must not worry.'

He nodded as he finished speaking, and there was a brief silence while Richard and Alice hugged their mother.

Kat and Nick were now feeling much happier since they knew they would soon have to be going home, and they didn't want to leave their friends in a desperate situation.

Kat had to break the news.

'We need to go back home... now,' she said, 'we don't want to leave, but our parents will be back before nightfall, and they will be worried about us if we're late turning up! We've quite a story to tell them!' she added. Richard smiled at her and waved as he moved away with the dispersing crowd. He and his mother were keen to see their new accommodation.

'Maybe we will see you tomorrow?' he shouted. 'Alice and I will come and find you!'

'Looking forward to it!' said Nick, though he knew that was not going to happen.

Alice wanted to walk to the top of the valley with Kat and Nick. She took a last look at the ashes and burnt timbers that were once her home. She shook her head but there was a smile on her face, as she knew the future looked a lot brighter than it had an hour ago. The three children walked along the river bank and then began the climb up the side of the valley. Nick wanted to ask something.

'Alice Fletcher, how is it that Clover the pig was living with you in your house?'

He laughed, finding the idea of having this animal sleeping so close to the family at night very strange, but it appealed to his sense of humour!

'Well, how would you like to sleep outside in winter?' Alice replied with a grin. 'And it's cheaper to let Clover share the house. Sometimes, there are chickens for company as well!

Anyway, I'd better be getting back to see how Richard and mother are doing.

I wonder where we're staying tonight - and what's for the evening meal! I'm ready for something to eat and a nice, long sleep. See you tomorrow!' She turned and skipped off down the slope, singing as she went. The children thought she seemed remarkably happy, considering the dramatic events of the day!

They carried on climbing until they reached the opening in the trees where their adventure had begun some hours ago. Glancing back at the cottages, they saw that renovation work had already begun, with debris being cleared by a multitude of willing helpers. At the rate they were working, it wouldn't be too long before new walls would be built and a new thatch attached. Then Richard, Alice, and their mother would be able to move in and begin a new chapter in their lives. The sun had come out again, and Tangleford Valley looked green and peaceful in its gentle light. Though they wanted to stay longer, the call of the magic path was urging the children to return to 2022.

They retraced their steps through trees and tall grasses until they reached the two felled tree trunks, which earlier had shown them the route to 1667 and now marked their way back home.

For a second, a chilly breeze rustled leaves on the trees around them, but when they stepped back onto the path, everywhere was still and warm in the pleasant sunshine. Both their phones showed it was 5.35 pm, which was close to the time when they had discovered Tangleford Valley. Their adventure must have lasted for several hours, but on this occasion, the path had brought them back home safely at the same time they had left, and it made no difference how long they had been away. Rain earlier on that day had made the path very muddy, and due to a carpet of wet oak leaves, its slippery surface had become far more tricky. The children proceeded with care and headed towards Kat's house. They talked about the events that had taken place that afternoon, but although they hoped that one day they would be able to share their secret, they promised each other they would keep it all to themselves for the time being.

'We're here!' shouted Kat as she opened her front door.

'Hi, Mr and Mrs Geraldson!' added Nick cheerily. He had just realised that he was ravenously hungry, and the smell of cooking food began to tantalise his taste buds!

'Come in, come in both, good timing, it's nearly six o'clock!' said Kat's Mum. 'And wash your hands, please! Tea is on the table very soon.'

Kat's dad appeared with a glass of beer in his hand. He was obviously feeling festive!

'We've got an early birthday surprise for you, Kat,' he said mysteriously. 'You can have it after tea!'

The children went upstairs to wash and make sure they were presentable for the meal.

The strong smell of smoke about them had somehow disappeared completely when they had joined the magic path, and so had the fire stains on their clothing!

Their T-shirts and jeans were every bit as clean as when they had put them on after school! They desperately wanted to continue talking about Tangleford Valley and their friends Richard and Alice, but Mum's voice calling out 'tea's ready' meant that conversation would have to be put on hold for the time being. Maybe after tea, they would surf the internet to find information about the valley in the mid sixteen hundreds – if it even existed!

Within minutes, they were sitting around the table, tucking into a large plateful of delicious chicken and chips!

There was a merry atmosphere as they ate and much laughter, especially when Dad accidentally squirted tomato sauce onto his new flowery shirt! They finished the main course and still had room for a chocolate cake topped with ice cream and raspberry sauce! There was one candle on the cake, which Dad lit, and Kat blew out for some early practice before the eleven she would have to deal with at tomorrow's party! When they had finally finished, he stood up and told Kat it was time for her 'early birthday surprise.'

'I went into town to buy your video game, Kat, and I saw that there was 50% off selected games,' he said, with some satisfaction. 'Legend of Legends' was included in the offer, so I bought it, along with another game I thought you'd like. Kind of two for the price of one!

You can have the Legend game tomorrow on your actual birthday, but here's something for today, just to whet your appetite!' He brought out a box from under the table. It was wrapped in paper covered in multicoloured balloons!

'Happy early birthday, love!' he said as he handed it to Kat. She took the box from her dad and excitedly tore the wrapping paper off. She saw the title and then took a sharp intake of breath before holding it up for Nick to read out loud. His mouth opened wide as he looked at the title. Then slowly, and with some amazement, he pronounced the words 'Plague and Fire - The Ultimate.'

Mum began wondering why the two children were suddenly so silent - speechless, for once!

'Well, we thought you'd be interested in this piece of history! The game is educational, besides being a lot of fun!' she said, as she took the box from Nick to have a look.

'After all, it's not as if you're ever going to witness it in person,' said Dad with a chuckle, 'it's too long ago, even for me to remember!' he added, trying unsuccessfully to be funny. Little did Kat's parents know just how far away they were from the truth. They waited for a response from the children. None was forthcoming.

Finally, Kat asked, 'Can we go and try it out, please?'

'Of course,' replied Mum. We'll do the washing up, won't we, Gerry?' she went on, winking at her husband, who agreed, although he rather fancied relaxing in a comfy armchair with the remainder of his drink.

Kat and Nick excused themselves from the table and disappeared into the front room. Her laptop was still in there on the coffee table, where she had left it that morning.

She loaded the game and mirrored it onto the big television so that they could get a better look.

What happened next was very strange indeed and took them completely by surprise. The intro began, and a voice-over explained the start of the game. The scene changed to show a sunlit valley, which had the same features as Tangleford Valley! Clips of the game came on, one by one. Kat paused the intro for a moment, slowly shaking her head with a look of bewilderment on her face. She briefly stared hard at Nick before they both

Secrets of the Magic Path | 45

turned back to the screen. Next, a boy and a girl appeared, walking down the valley towards several thatched cottages. In fields on the other side of a river, men and women were going about their daily work. A frightened horse galloped into the picture, pursued by two men, anxious to catch it. Tasks had to be carried out before the children could reach the thatched cottages. The picture then zoomed in to show a close-up of the first cottage, which had the number 1647 painted on a board over the door!

As the intro progressed, two other children came to meet them and invited them into the dim interior. They were taken to see a man lying on a bed, his eyes closed and looking extremely ill. Posies of flowers lay on a table next to him. All four of them had to go and look for herbs in the valley that would make a potion to cure his illness.

The scene changed from plague to fire as the next clip flicked back to show two of the cottages ablaze. More tasks had to be undertaken to rescue people and animals from the flames.

To finish the game, all the fires had to be extinguished and the cottages rebuilt, returning the hamlet to relative peace. Incredibly, 'Plague And Fire – The Ultimate' closely matched many of Kat and Nick's recent experiences in Tangleford Valley!

The two children sat together for a moment longer, watching the credits on the television screen. When the company and creators' names came up, they saw that the game was produced by 'Galahad Entertainment,' but even more astounding were the names of the designers and developers – 'Alice and Richard Fletcher'!

This had to be a massive coincidence! Or maybe it was yet another twist, engineered by the magic path, subtly teasing the children at the end of their adventure and gently reminding them of its extraordinary powers!

Kat closed the video game down and disconnected the laptop from the television. She, Nick, and the laptop then headed for the quiet upstairs, where they would have a further opportunity to continue discussions on their recent experiences and also be able to explore 'Plague and Fire' from start to finish without being disturbed!

Their overriding wish, however, was to be presented with another chance to discover more of the unknown secrets of the magic path. There was no certainty that they would ever find another entrance to a different part of the past or maybe even the future. There was no guarantee that they would, at some point, be given the slightest hint of their next destination or whoever they were to meet. Having now had three visits to contrasting eras, they were filled with the spirit of adventure, but for the time being, there were other pressing commitments to occupy them both. Though this day had been yet another special one to remember and treasure, the excitement wasn't over yet, as there was the little matter of Kat's birthday celebrations, and these were only just beginning!

Secrets of the Magic Path | 49